Some reader comments on the first Tattoo Fox book

Now I can make my Granddaughter happy, by telling her that the sequel is here!
QUINTIN JARDINE

Reading this book right now, next time I go to Edinburgh I will be looking for the wee fox
SANDRA VIDLER

Great book, lovely little story. The pictures my brain was dreaming up – I was there xxx
KATE HOBSON

I purchased this book while on holiday in Edinburgh last August. Sat in Princes Street Gardens and had a wee read. Great book I love it!!! Even though I'm an older child (by quite a few years!!!)
JANE BROWN

The book is fantastic, well worth buying for children and adults, I really enjoyed the book
SUSAN GIBSON

It is a lovely book, good story
DOROTHY JARRETT

My wee girl bought the book the night we were at the Tattoo and she has read it and loved it. My older boy, he has read it and loved it. Now, I'm 3/4 way through it! Can't wait until I go to bed to finish it tonight, lovely wee book. Please, please do another one!
DEHRA HIGGINSON

Brigadier David Allfrey MBE
Chief Executive and Producer
The Royal Edinburgh Military Tattoo

We have been thrilled by the success of The Tattoo Fox and have enjoyed the whole adventure. We have been fortunate to come together with a fun and efficient team at Luath who have guided us through the process and past the pitfalls. Since the launch at the Edinburgh International Book Festival last year, we have received many wonderful and uplifting comments from adults and children, all praising Alasdair's writing and Stref's illustrations – a winning combination.

With the Tattoo, a 400-year-old Castle, the City of Edinburgh and Scotland as a backdrop, it has been easy to imagine what our fox might have been up to over the last 12 months. Stories abound – both apocryphal and real – of foxy encounters in the Castle precincts. So, with phone calls to the author, illustrator, editor and our publishers, the stage was easily set for *The Tattoo Fox Makes New Friends*.

We are hugely proud to now present our second book just as the Royal Edinburgh Military Tattoo starts its 65th season and a 15th sell-out season. We know the fox, her family and her friends will be watching our show and enjoying the festival atmosphere. I hope you enjoy this second set of stories as much as we have.

yours aye

David

August 2014

THE
TATTOO FOX
MAKES NEW
FRIENDS

by Alasdair Hutton

with illustrations by Stref

Luath Press Limited
EDINBURGH
www.luath.co.uk

First published 2014

ISBN: 978-1-910021-47-7

The paper used in this book is recyclable. It is made
from low chlorine pulps produced in a low energy, low emission
manner from renewable forests.

Printed and bound by
CPI Group (UK) Ltd, Croydon, CR0 4YY

Typeset in 11.5 point Din

The Royal Edinburgh Military Tattoo was established for charitable
purposes to support services and artistic charities. In recent years we
have disbursed several million pounds.

Each year we stage a world-class event from which a
substantial amount is Gift Aided to The Royal Edinburgh Military
Tattoo Charities Ltd which is then dispersed as donations to a range
of charitable organisations.

If you enjoy the book then please give a thought to our charitable
purposes and perhaps make a donation, join our Friends or become
a supporter. Find out more at **www.edintattoo.co.uk**

The Edinburgh Military Tattoo (Charities) Ltd is a company limited by
guarantee Registered in Scotland No. 108857. Charity No. SC018377.

Patron: HRH The Princess Royal, Princess Anne

Contents

Thanks   7

Chapter One
The Fox takes a Trip   9

Chapter Two
The Long Walk Home   17

Chapter Three
Trains and Planes and Suitcases   26

Chapter Four
Edinburgh Ghosts!   35

Chapter Five
Operation Dog Rescue   45

Chapter Six
The Roaring Crowd and a Noble Penguin   53

Chapter Seven
A Magical Mystery Tour   62

Chapter Eight
Five!   73

Chapter Nine
Underground Hide and Seek   84

Chapter Ten
Another Castle, Another Time   94

Chapter Eleven
The Uninvited Guests   102

Chapter Twelve
A Party to Remember   113

Thanks

After the first book about the Tattoo Fox was published in 2013, it was a very pleasant surprise to be asked to write some more of the adventures of this little animal who lives on Edinburgh Castle Rock.

It takes many more people than the writer to make any story successful and once again the incomparable and inspirational Lindsey Fraser has turned the first rough garment into an elegant cloak to be proud of with her skilful editing.

Stref's superb drawings have brought the little tales to life and made them much more enjoyable and the pictures on the front and back covers are more vibrant thanks to Fin Cramb's remarkable dexterity with colours.

In the Tattoo office, Nancy Riach diplomatically made sure everyone stuck to the timetable so that these stories would be ready for the 2014 Tattoo, and the Producer, Brigadier David Allfrey, who started the whole idea, was enthusiastically encouraging at every stage.

The staff of the publishers, Luath Press, in particular Gavin MacDougall and Lydia Nowak, were constantly positive and helpful in making this book a reality.

Thanks to Morris Heggie from DC Thomson for wisdom and support.

Any failings in the book are mine alone but everyone involved has been so helpful and enthusiastic that I cannot thank them enough and hope you will enjoy reading more of these little tales about the Tattoo Fox.

1

The Fox takes a Trip

The fox and cat go off to roam
And find they have a long trip home

The Royal Edinburgh Military Tattoo was over for another year.

Sparkling fireworks soared into the sky above Edinburgh Castle for the last time, the bands marched away down the Royal Mile and the pipes and drums fell silent at last.

On the final night, the Tattoo Fox had joined the parade down the Esplanade. As she padded past the Producer, her magnificent tail waving proudly, he smiled. 'Bravo, Tattoo Fox. I hope I see you here next year.'

Once the audience had gone home the Tattoo Fox stood beneath the stands thinking about the excitement of the last three weeks. It was there that her friend the Castle Cat found her.

'You looked spectacular tonight,' he said, 'and you got an especially loud cheer at the end. You must have felt like the Queen.'

'I was very proud,' the fox admitted. 'I'm sorry it's over until next summer.' The Castle Cat had promised her that the Royal Edinburgh Military Tattoo would be an experience she would never forget. And he was right.

They watched some musicians loading oddly-shaped boxes into the back of a big van.

'They're from the Band of Her Majesty's Royal Marines,' said the Castle Cat. 'I wonder what they're up to...'

'Fancy a cup of tea?' one of the Marines called to his friends after some particularly heavy lifting. 'Thought you'd never ask! I'm thirsty after all that blowing,' said another. They headed up the Esplanade towards the Castle.

'Super!' said the Castle Cat. Like most cats, he couldn't resist looking in boxes. He ran out from under the stands and leapt in the back of the van. The fox followed and the two of them had a lovely time nosing their way round. The boxes came in all shapes and sizes. 'I wonder what lives in this one?' the fox said, puzzling over how to open it. But before she could find out, there was

a rumbling noise and a click as the shutter of the van was rolled down and locked. The two friends were left in total darkness.

'Off you go!' they heard one of the Marines call. 'See you back at the base.' There was a shudder as the van's engine started, and then it started to move.

'Oh, no!' said the fox, staggering from side to side. 'Where are we going? My family expects me home...'

'There is nothing we can do until the van stops,' said the Castle Cat sensibly. 'We might as well settle down and make ourselves comfortable until then.'

As they rattled along the cat snoozed, but the fox was too worried to sleep. Her heart was thumping as she lay as flat as she could, desperate for the journey to end, hoping the boxes wouldn't tumble on top of her.

At last the van slowed and stopped, the engine idling. They could hear shouts of friendly greetings, and then they set off again for a short distance. When the engine was turned off they could hear people moving about outside. Soon the shutter was unlocked and pushed up a little way.

'There are quite a few instruments to unpack,' said one of the Marines, peering in. 'Let's go and find some willing helpers. Might have to wake a few of them up...'

The two friends did not need to think twice. As soon as the Marine's back was turned, the fox and the cat jumped out and headed towards the darkness. 'Do you have any idea where we are?' the fox asked as they crouched beneath a bush. They could make out quite a few vans and several low buildings, some of them with lights on.

'No,' the cat said. He had no idea, and was trying not to sound worried.

'What should we do next?' asked the fox. 'I must get home!'

'So must I,' agreed the cat. 'But we can't just set off into the blue yonder until we know where we are. We might head off in completely the wrong direction, and then where would we be? We might even end up in... Glasgow!' He shook himself violently. 'That would never do.' He sniffed the air for a moment. 'Let's go this way,' he said finally.

They slipped silently beneath trees and bushes, from shadow to shadow until they were well away from the buildings, then scampered up a steep slope. Below them they could see a huge dark space, and the lights of what looked like a big ship.

'Where are we?' the fox asked again.

'Can't be sure,' the cat replied, his tail twitching, 'but that dark space might be the Firth of Forth – the water that separates Edinburgh from the Kingdom of Fife. We can sometimes see it from the Castle. If I'm right we need to cross it to get back home.'

The fox had never swum in her life. Her heart began thumping again. She wondered whether the Castle Cat was a keen swimmer. After they'd walked a bit further she asked, 'What are those red lights blinking in the sky?'

The Castle Cat bounded over to have a better look. 'That, my friend, is the Forth Road Bridge.' He purred triumphantly. 'Those lights show pilots coming to land at Edinburgh Airport where the bridge is. I know exactly where we are now. We are at Rosyth where the Marine musicians are

based. Those boxes were for their trombones and clarinets and trumpets and saxophones. That's why they were all different shapes.' He was very relieved.

'But how far are we from Edinburgh Castle?' asked the fox anxiously.

'Not far. In fact, when the sun comes up we may be able to see Edinburgh Castle in the distance,' said the Castle Cat. 'But for now, let's catch supper and have a rest. It's been a long day, and we have quite a journey ahead of us.'

2

The Long Walk Home

**The friends head home but don't quite know
Which is the best way they should go**

The Castle Cat was quite right. The van that drove him and the Tattoo Fox from Edinburgh Castle had taken them to the Caledonia base at Rosyth on the north shore of the Firth of Forth. In the morning, they watched men and women coming and going on the base, all wearing naval uniforms. They looked very purposeful.

'I know you want to get home but what with traffic and dangerous dogs, it really is better to wait until after dark,' said the cat.

The Tattoo Fox knew her friend was right. She tried not to think about the long swim ahead. But as the day wore on, she could think of little else. When daylight faded she led the Castle Cat to a shallow scrape in the ground under the fence. 'I think local foxes must have made this,' she said, sniffing the ground. She slunk under the fence and the cat followed.

They made their way carefully past rows of houses, ducking into gardens when they heard voices, or when cars drove too close. 'If we keep those red blinking lights on the Forth Road Bridge in our sights we'll be fine,' the Castle Cat said. 'Luckily it's a clear night.' Finally, they came to a road that was far too broad and busy for them to cross. Cars and lorries roared by, one after the other, their headlights dazzling. The noise was deafening.

'Stick with me,' said the cat, staying close to the gorse bushes by the side of the road. At last they found themselves looking along the Forth Road Bridge. It was enormous – even broader than the Esplanade at the Castle.

'We'll use this walkway,' explained the Castle Cat. 'There won't be anybody walking across the bridge in the middle of the night.'

The fox turned to him. 'Walkway?' she repeated. 'Aren't we going to swim?'

'Don't be ridiculous!' said the cat. 'I make it a rule never, *ever* to go near water. And if you have any sense, you'll stick to that rule too. Is that clear?'

'Absolutely!' replied the fox. She was so relieved.

'The walkway was built for walking,' the cat said. He gave her a long hard look. 'There will be no swimming, my friend.'

'Of course not,' said the fox, and she followed him onto the bridge. A very long way beneath the walkway she could see the choppy waters of the Firth of Forth. She decided it was better to keep looking straight ahead.

At the midway point on the bridge, the Castle Cat stopped. 'It's quite a climb, isn't it?'

'We're very high up,' said the fox a little nervously. 'Are you sure this is the right bridge?' There was another one, all lit up not far away.

'That is the Forth Railway Bridge,' said the cat. 'That's for trains.'

'And what's that?' asked the fox. To their right they could see huge pillars in the water.

'That must be the new bridge,' said the cat.

'What a lot of bridges for one river,' said the fox. She was rather impressed.

It was easier going downhill towards South Queensferry, until suddenly, as if from nowhere, burst a flashing white light. It grew bigger, and brighter.

The fox was used to making herself scarce, and she pressed herself into the railings. The cat was not used to making himself scarce and he froze, terrified. The white light was almost on top of him when they heard a screeching of brakes. A late night cyclist! The man blinked, wobbled and stopped just in time. 'Well I never!' he cried. 'Wildlife on the Forth Road Bridge!'

'Run!' The Tattoo Fox circled the cat. 'Hurry!'

Finally, although he was rather insulted at being called 'wildlife', the cat recovered himself and set off faster than the fox had ever seen him move.

Once off the bridge, they kept up their pace along the main road, slipping past houses and hotels and offices until finally they ran through an open gateway. Only when they found a large rhododendron bush to hide under did they stop.

'What a ridiculous time to be cycling across the Forth Road Bridge,' huffed the Castle Cat. 'I might have fallen off the walkway into the water!' He shuddered.

'But you didn't,' soothed the fox. 'Let's count our blessings and find our bearings.'

'The sign at the gate said 'Dundas Castle',' the cat said. 'Well, castles are usually civilised places. In fact, I'm sure one of my second cousins lived here at one time,' he added.

They padded up a long drive lined with more rhododendron bushes. 'This must be lovely in springtime,' the fox said. 'But... *shhh...*' The hackles rose along her back. The cat's eyes widened, and without a word the friends slipped out of sight and waited.

22

The fox's instinct was right. They had been spotted. A large and handsome fox trotted over and took a good look at them. 'And what do you think you're doing in there?' he asked. His tone was wary but not unfriendly. 'Is that a... cat?'

'It's the Castle Cat,' said the Tattoo Fox carefully.

'Really? *I'm* the Castle Fox! The Dundas Castle Fox, to give me my full name. Do come out and introduce yourselves.'

The friends emerged. 'We're trying to get home to Edinburgh Castle. Can you tell us the quickest route? I live in the Castle buildings,' explained the Castle Cat rather grandly, 'and my friend lives with her family in a den on the Castle Rock. She was the star of this year's Royal Edinburgh Military Tattoo, don't you know. She's known as the Tattoo Fox.'

'I have heard of the Edinburgh Tattoo but I've never been,' said the Castle Fox.

'You would love it,' said the Tattoo Fox. 'Why don't you come next summer? Everybody should see the Edinburgh Tattoo!' Her hackles were down. The Dundas Castle Fox was definitely a friend.

'That would be wonderful,' he said. Then he looked down the driveway. 'But I need to warn you that there's a large wedding party going on. We have weddings here most weekends. Such a fuss... and far too many cars. Let's go this-away.'

He led his guests to a good hunting spot where they enjoyed a meal together. Then he carefully explained the route to Edinburgh. 'I must go,' he said, once he was sure they had everything they needed. 'It was a great pleasure to meet such distinguished visitors and I look forward to the Tattoo next August.'

'What a very nice fellow,' the Castle Cat said, watching their host trotting back down the driveway. Then he curled up under a bush, yawned and settled down to sleep.

3

Trains and Planes and Suitcases

**The Airport is a magic sight
But gives the Fox a dreadful fright**

The Castle Cat slept soundly, but the Tattoo Fox didn't. As soon as it was light, she woke him and although he was a little grumpy, they set off, following the Dundas Castle Fox's directions towards a nearby railway line. He had told them they might be able to see Edinburgh Castle from there. They climbed the bank and peered into the morning mist.

Suddenly from behind them came a harsh metallic noise, and the ground beneath their paws began to rumble and shake. A train roared past with a rush of wind so violent that the cat lost his balance and rolled down the bank. The fox bounded after him, relieved to find her friend upright and uninjured at the bottom – but shaken.

'This is a dangerous place,' the cat said. His ears were very flat.

At the top of another slope, they could see the Pentland Hills and even Edinburgh Castle perched high on its rock. So they were definitely heading in the right direction. They padded on. For a while all was calm, but suddenly there was a new noise, this time from above. It was a loud roaring sound, like a high wind. The two friends crouched low in the grass until it faded.

'Whatever was that?' The fox was trembling.

'I think it was an aircraft landing,' said the Castle Cat. 'Didn't the Castle Fox mention that his route took us near Edinburgh Airport?' The friends had spent many an evening on the castle ramparts watching planes swooping through the Edinburgh skies on their way to the airport. But they'd never heard an engine noise as loud as that.

'Lots of the performers at the Tattoo travel by plane. I think we should take a look at the airport, don't you?' suggested the Castle Cat. 'Things can't possibly get any noisier.'

The fox was relieved to see her friend in better spirits after the horrible experience with the train, so she agreed to his plan. She too was a curious creature. Beneath a high wire fence she sniffed out a shallow scrape. On the other side they found themselves in a huge field with a long road down the middle. A road with no cars.

The fox began to ask what it was, but her question was drowned out by the shattering noise of yet another huge aircraft sweeping low above their heads. With a deafening screech of its massive wheels it touched down on the wide road and raced towards a long building in the distance. The fox quivered with fright. 'Was it aiming for us?'

'Worry not,' said the Castle Cat. 'It was aiming for the runway – you're quite safe.'

Every few minutes another plane landed on the runway before taxi-ing to a halt. The fox still jumped at the noise, but not as much as the first time. Nearer the airport, men and women wearing yellow waistcoats unloaded suitcases from a little truck. They heaved them on to a moving belt which carried them through a plastic curtain out of sight.

Forgetting the trouble they'd landed in the last time they'd gone to investigate something, the two friends scampered across and jumped on to the moving belt, crouching as flat as they could next to two bright pink suitcases.

It wasn't long before they realised that they were in big trouble.

Inside the baggage hall, passengers were waiting to collect their cases, tired after their long flight. At first they thought they were dreaming when a magnificent fox and an enormous grey cat appeared through the curtains along with the cases.

'Is that... a *fox*?' asked a smart businesswoman, pointing.

'And that's definitely a cat,' said her friend.

'Are they stowaways?' suggested somebody else. 'Should we call security?'

The fox and the cat gripped the moving belt, not sure where and when to jump off.

But before they could decide, a little girl pointed at them, smiling. 'Mummy! It's the fox from Edinburgh Castle, the one who found me!'
It was the little girl with golden curls who had lost her parents one day at Edinburgh Castle. The fox had helped reunite them.

'Yes, Aline,' said her mother. 'I'm sure it is. Take my hand and we'll go and find Daddy.' She wasn't really paying attention.

The little girl waved as the fox and the cat disappeared back through the plastic curtain along with all the unclaimed luggage. The minute they were outside, the two friends leapt off and escaped round the corner of the building. One of the baggage handlers started to make chase, but she soon gave up, laughing.

The fox followed the cat in the direction of a tall slender building shaped like an hour glass. 'That's the Control Tower,' he explained as they ran towards a half open gate which led them towards some covering bushes and away from the buildings. 'The people in there know all there is to know about every flight landing or taking off from Edinburgh Airport. Keep running!' Soon they were looking down onto the tram depot.

'Why don't we jump on board?' the fox suggested. She had seen trams trundling along Princes Street.

'Let's just use our own four legs,' said the cat. He wasn't a big fan of the trams.

'We must be nearly home now,' said the cat, after a while. 'I can see Murrayfield stadium. It's empty now but in six months' time it'll be packed with people.'

'Like the Tattoo?' asked the fox.

'About sixty thousand people pack it out for really important rugby matches,' her friend explained. 'That's even more than come to the Tattoo every night.'

'It sounds like fun,' the fox declared.

The cat looked doubtful. 'If you thought those planes were noisy, you should hear the roar of a Murrayfield crowd.'

The two friends were very tired and their paws were sore when they slipped into Princes Street Gardens and climbed the Castle rock. When they reached the den the fox gave a little bark and the dog fox looked out. 'At last!' he said. The kits rushed out to greet their mother. 'Where have you been?' they fussed.

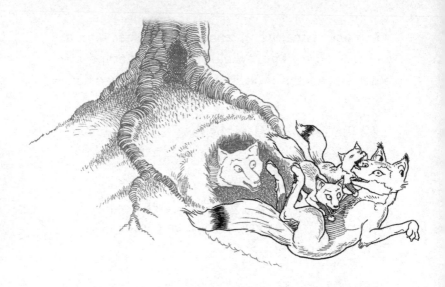

'Good night,' said the Castle Cat, satisfied that his friend was safely reunited with her family. 'I am off for a long sleep. I hope the soldiers have saved some titbits for me.' He yawned, leapt up the last few rocks and vanished between the railings into the night.

4

Edinburgh Ghosts!

The little foxes like the night
And give a ghost an awful fright

Like all fox kits the Tattoo Fox's kits were curious about everything and they couldn't wait to start exploring. 'When can we go?' they demanded, day after day.

One clear frosty night while the dog fox was out hunting, the Tattoo Fox decided it was time for an expedition. She made the kits promise they wouldn't leave her side, and led them up the steep rock and through the railings onto the Esplanade of Edinburgh Castle. The cars and buses and visitors had gone home for the day so the three animals ran unnoticed towards the Royal Mile.

At the top of Castlehill the Tattoo Fox flicked her tail with alarm. 'Where's your brother? He was here only a second ago!' she growled, her coat bristling.

'Surprise!' The little fox skipped out from behind a statue. 'Scared you, didn't I?' he said proudly.

'Please don't ever do that again,' his mother said sharply. 'Who knows what might have happened? You must stay close!'

'I was just playing Hide and Seek,' the little fox said, abashed.

'Look!' said the smaller kit. She had stopped by a little fountain set into the wall. 'I see a snake!'

'And a foxglove,' observed her brother.

'It commemorates a terrible time hundreds of years ago when women who people decided were witches were killed. Look – you can see two heads, one looks evil and the other looks

good. That's to show that some people use their powers for good, and others don't,' explained the fox. 'Thank goodness they don't hunt witches or warlocks these days.' She gave a little shiver, and set off. The kits stayed close behind her as they darted down Castlehill and across the top of Johnston Terrace.

'Will we see witches tonight?' asked one of the kits as they ran down towards the West Bow.

'No,' said the fox firmly. 'There are no witches in Edinburgh. Though there are quite a few ghosts. And there are people who don't much like foxes,' she added as she led the kits further down the hill.

Suddenly the kits stopped in their tracks, their brushes standing up like flagpoles and their noses twitching. A tall thin figure wrapped in a dark cloak with a white face was pacing towards them.

'A ghost!' chattered the dog kit, and they all ducked into the shadow of a shop doorway, making themselves as invisible as they could. The footsteps came closer and the foxes held their breath, but the man tramped on without seeing them, muttering to himself about the cold.

The Tattoo Fox nudged the kits back onto the pavement. 'Don't worry,' she said. 'That is just somebody pretending to be a ghost. It's his job to give visitors to Edinburgh a fright. After the visitors get over the shock, that man will tell them stories about Edinburgh long ago.'

'What stories?' asked the kits.

Their mother thought for a moment. Then she twitched her tail, remembering her favourite. She hoped it wouldn't give them nightmares. 'There was a man who lived near here in the Grassmarket who was a respectable citizen by day – but a thief at night. His name was Deacon William Brodie. Deacon Brodie was an expert at making furniture and repairing locks. But what his customers didn't know was that he always made copies of the keys to the locks he was repairing.'

'That's very crafty,' said the smaller kit.

'At night he would use his duplicate keys to break into his customers' houses and rob them.'

'That's not crafty – that's nasty,' said the other kit.

'Oh, he didn't get away with it forever,' the Tattoo Fox assured them. 'He was caught and hanged. Some people say that if you listen carefully at night you can hear his ghost, jingling his keys... roaming the streets of Edinburgh.'

The kits stared at her.

'Don't worry,' she added quickly. 'It's probably just a silly story.'

The Grassmarket was almost empty now apart from a few party-goers carefully making their way home. 'One of the Castle Cat's favourite authors – Robert Louis Stevenson – wrote a book based on Deacon Brodie. It's called *The Strange Case of Dr Jekyll and Mr Hyde*,' the Tattoo Fox said as they scampered along. 'People from all over the world read it.'

'I can hear jingling,' squeaked one of the kits after a few moments, and they all stopped to listen. 'I'm sure...'

'You're imagining it,' his mother said gently.

But then the kit's ears twitched again. 'Listen!' he insisted. 'It must be the ghost of Deacon Brodie! And he's coming this way...'

The foxes ducked into a bookshop. Striding towards them was another figure wearing a long dark cloak, but this one was wearing a top hat. He carried a staff and marched along like a soldier. And he was definitely jingling.

'Stay low,' instructed the fox.

But the man was in a hurry, he didn't even lift his eyes from the pavement. And in his hand he carried a set of keys.

'It *must* be Deacon Brodie!' chattered one of the kits.

The Tattoo Fox felt the fur on her back start to rise. She shivered ever so slightly. It was time they were heading for the safety of the den – and supper. Once the man was out of sight she urged the kits on, her nose twitching and her ears flicking.

On Victoria Street a group of tourists stood gawping at the height of the tenements. 'I'm sure one of the guides said there were eleven layers,' said one of them. 'I suppose they're prototypes of the New York City skyscrapers back home.' The tourists were so busy looking upwards that they didn't notice the three foxes speeding by.

On Castlehill the foxes almost caught up with the man with the jingling keys. All of a sudden he slipped into one of the narrow closes and leant against the wall. Waiting. The kits chattered with alarm.

'Leave well alone,' warned their mother.

But the kits looked at each other. They had other ideas. 'Oh no you *don't*, Deacon Brodie!' They crept up behind the man and tugged hard at his cloak, almost pulling him over, then, just as the tourists arrived they ran away.

The Tattoo Fox yipped in alarm, but the naughty kits were already back by her side by the time the

man ran out into the street, jingling his keys and shouting, 'Ghosts! I've been attacked by a ghost! It tried to yank my cloak from my back!'

'A ghost stealing from a ghost!' The tourists burst out laughing.

The pretend ghost began to laugh too – once he was over the shock. He hitched his cloak back onto his shoulders and began to tell his stories. But none of the tourists could take him very seriously now.

The three foxes slipped away up the Esplanade and through the railings, pleased to have played their part in proving that Edinburgh really is the most haunted city in Europe.

5

Operation Dog Rescue

**The fox and kits go on a tour
And free a dog who's held secure**

One fine moonlit winter night the Tattoo Fox
led the kits up the rock onto the Esplanade and
slipped through the gates into a large tunnel.
'This is how big trucks and fire engines enter
Edinburgh Castle,' she explained.

Happy to have the place to themselves, the kits
ran back and forth along the Argyle Battery
with its row of cast iron guns looking out at the
twinkling city lights below. 'Come on!' called their
mother and led them up the Lang Stairs. At the
top she trotted towards an enormous siege gun.

'Oooh,' said the kits, their eyes wide. 'Is that what makes the big bang every day at one o'clock?'

'No,' said their mother.

'No, indeed,' said a familiar voice. The Castle Cat was on one of his evening wanders. 'This gun is more than five hundred years old,' he explained. 'But the barrel burst more than three hundred years ago and it has not been fired since.' He leapt on top of the gun. He loved showing off his knowledge of the history of Edinburgh Castle. 'This is Mons Meg. It was a present to King James the Second in the fifteenth century. But it was far too heavy to be any use.' The cat jumped down again. 'For many years it was kept in the Tower

46

of London, but Sir Walter Scott – another of my favourite authors – arranged for it to be returned here in 1829. This is the perfect place for it. It's the highest point in the Castle and the views are magnificent, even at night.'

'Who lives here?' asked one of the kits, skipping over to a doorway.

The Castle Cat turned. 'This is Saint Margaret's Chapel, the oldest building in the Castle, even older than Mons Meg. It was built early in the twelfth century and although it has been used for many other things over the years, it is a chapel again now.'

Headlights suddenly dazzled in the darkness. The kits ran towards their mother. She had warned them well about the danger of cars.

'Let's tuck ourselves away in these bushes,' said the cat. A moment later several large vehicles drove past and disappeared round the corner. 'There must be something happening in the Great Hall tonight,' said the cat. 'Wait here while

I go and see what it is.' He strolled off round the corner.

In the distance they heard a dog barking, The Tattoo Fox's ears twitched. The kits nestled close. They didn't like dogs very much.

At last the Castle Cat returned. 'There's a concert in the Great Hall,' he explained. 'I heard bagpipes tuning up. Rather a smart affair, and if we're careful, we could slip in and hear it.'

One of the kits was so excited that he did a perfect somersault. The Tattoo Fox cuffed him gently. 'Behave...' she whispered.

The cat led the way through the shadows along the edge of Crown Square. When no-one was watching, he ushered the foxes through the rear door of the Great Hall and up to the gallery. From there they peered through the decorative woodwork. A choir of schoolchildren, standing in front of the great fireplace, sang a selection of Scottish folk songs. Although they were used to the sound of the bagpipes, the kits didn't like the noisy applause and at the interval they all slipped out into the cool evening air of the square again.

'Over there is the Royal Palace where the Scottish Crown Jewels are kept,' the Castle Cat told them.

'Can we see them?' asked one of the kits.

'Don't be silly,' said the other, 'they're locked up at night.'

'I hear that dog barking again,' said the smaller kit. She ran to her mother.

'But it's not exactly barking,' said the Tattoo Fox. 'It's more like whimpering.'

They stood, listening.

'It sounds like a dog in a spot of bother,' said the Castle Cat finally. 'Somebody needs our help.' He didn't like dogs any more than the foxes did but he couldn't ignore the sound of an animal in trouble.

'I think it's coming from this direction.' He padded smartly towards the old vaults and it wasn't long before they found a small Border Terrier with a red collar trapped in a thick roll of wire netting. Her head was twisted to one side. 'I'm in such a pickle,' she said in a small voice. 'Please can you help? I promise I won't yap or nip.'

The foxes hung back while the cat investigated. 'Ah...' he said finally. 'Your identity tag is trapped in the netting. We'll have you free in no time. Don't worry,' the cat added. 'I'm the Castle Cat and this is the Tattoo Fox and her fine family. Utterly trustworthy, I assure you.' As he puzzled over how to untangle the netting, he added, 'Is this your first visit to Edinburgh Castle? What is your name?'

'Myrtle,' replied the little dog. 'My mistress is at the concert. She always leaves the car window open so that I don't overheat. I like to go exploring, but as usual my nose got the better of me. Somebody must have dropped a sandwich. I've a soft spot for cheese and pickle. I'll never learn...'

Under the Castle Cat's direction, the fox kits pulled at the wire netting until, with a ping, the tag came free and the little dog reversed carefully out. 'I can't thank you enough,' she said, gingerly stretching her neck. Once they were sure that there was no injury, the five animals set off down the cobbled hill.

'Myrtle is a pretty name. Where does it come from?' asked the cat.

'The myrtle is my mistress's favourite flower,' replied the terrier. 'It's the symbol of honour in ancient Greece. Myrtle leaves were used to make the wreaths for the winners of the first Olympic Games.'

The Castle Cat was impressed. More fascinating facts to add to his collection.

At the Jacobite restaurant, the kits jumped on to a large gun. 'Down!' scolded the Tattoo Fox. 'That's the One o'Clock Gun.' She wanted to show Myrtle and the Castle Cat that she knew some fascinating facts too. 'We hear it every day, except for Sundays.'

The kits scampered ahead, down the road and over the drawbridge. On the Castle Esplanade was a neat row of cars. Myrtle headed for the silver one. 'This is my mistress's car,' she said. 'I can wait for her here. Thank you again.' I've so enjoyed meeting you.'

'Come back in the summer and watch the Tattoo with us,' the Fox said. 'I'm having a party.'

'I've heard the Tattoo fireworks from home but I've never actually been,' Myrtle said. 'I would love to come!'

'I'm looking forward to my Tattoo party,' said the fox with a spring in her step as they made for home.

6

The Roaring Crowd and a Noble Penguin

The fox cheers on the men in blue
Then finds a new friend at the Zoo

The winter was far from over when the Castle Cat invited the Tattoo Fox to join him at a rugby match at Murrayfield Stadium the following Saturday. They set off at dawn to avoid the crowds. Before long they reached the stadium gates and trotted through the tunnel leading to the famous rugby pitch. There were a few people checking the seating or making last-minute tweaks to the turf. Nobody noticed a fox and a cat in such a vast space.

'This is huge,' whispered the fox.

'It's the Calcutta Cup today, there won't be a single empty seat,' said the cat. 'We might need to watch from the roof! But first let's have a run on the hallowed Murrayfield turf. Come on!' The Castle Cat was a keen follower of rugby. The two friends ran onto the grass and scampered towards what looked like an enormous letter H. 'If we make it over the line, we've scored a try for Scotland!'

But suddenly there was an angry shout and the friends veered left and escaped down the nearest tunnel and up a set of stairs. 'That was a narrow squeak,' said the cat.

'Yes, but fun,' said the fox, her eyes shining. 'Let's find somewhere near the pitch to watch the match. Then we can slip away at the end before the crowds leave.' Back downstairs again, they found the perfect spot next to the low wall surrounding the pitch. Comfortable and completely hidden, they settled down and fell asleep.

They were wakened by a growing noise. The stadium was filling up with rugby fans of all shapes and sizes, finding their seats and greeting their friends. Some of them clapped in time to the military band playing on the pitch. The fox and the

cat took up their positions just as a mighty roar broke out from all over the stadium. The England team, all in white, ran on to the pitch, bouncing up and down, stretching their necks and looking fantastically fierce.

Then an even louder cheer rose from the stands as the home team, dressed in blue, ran out. They too bounced and stretched, loosening their muscles in preparation for the match. After a few moments, the stadium quietened and the crowd sang the two anthems. Then the referee blew the whistle – and the match began.

The noise was louder and went on longer than the train and all the planes the friends had encountered put together. All around the stadium people roared their support for the brave players. Play surged from end to end and the score was very close. By the time the final whistle blew, both teams were muddy and exhausted, battered and bruised. It had been a splendid game.

But the fox and the cat were so absorbed that they missed their chance to leave before the crowds. 'This is my worst nightmare,' muttered the fox. But she knew she had to be brave. Finally the friends managed to wind their way through thousands of legs until they found the little bridge leading over the Water of Leith into the streets and gardens of Saughtonhall.

'We are very close to Edinburgh Zoo,' said the cat. 'It must be closing time soon, and I'd love to introduce you to one of my oldest friends. By the time we've done that, the rugby crowds will have gone.'

Glad of some peace and quiet, the fox followed
the cat through a side gate to Edinburgh Zoo and
they hid in the bushes while the last of the visitors
were leaving. Then they sped up the hill.

'These are not friends of mine,' said the Castle Cat
as they passed the African Painted Hunting Dogs.
'I wouldn't trust them as far as I could throw them.'

The Tattoo Fox wondered how far the cat could
have thrown one of those handsome creatures,
but decided not to ask. 'They don't look in the
least like Myrtle,' she said instead. 'I've never
seen birds like these around the Castle,' she
observed a few moments later. Their long legs
were so spindly that she didn't know how they
supported their plump pink bodies and their large
black beaks. 'And I've never seen anything like
those either,' she said, as they passed two black
and white bears.

'Those are Giant Pandas,' said the cat
knowledgeably. 'They come from China and I do
not think they speak our language.'

'Hello, Giant Pandas,' called the fox.

The pandas looked puzzled.

'You're right,' she said, and trotted on.

There was a sudden whiff of fish and water. 'Here we are,' said the cat brightly. 'Time to meet a very fine fellow.'

The fox was surprised that any friend of the Castle Cat's would live near water. But there was a good reason.

'Welcome to Edinburgh Zoo's famous penguins and – over there – the most famous penguin of them all, Sir Nils Olav.'

The important-looking penguin waddled over and the Castle Cat made the introductions.

'Welcome!' said Sir Nils. 'And why are you called the Tattoo Fox?'

The fox explained and Sir Nils clapped his flippers at the description of her marching with the bands.

'I love it! And funnily enough, I am here because of the Tattoo although I have never been. I was adopted many years ago by the Norwegian King's Guard, and every time they come back to perform at the Tattoo they promote me because of my long service and good conduct. That is why I am called *Sir* Nils Olav, an honour approved by King Harald himself. And, as a matter of fact, I am now the Commander in Chief of the Norwegian Armed Forces,' he added proudly.

'Please come and watch the Tattoo with us next year!' The fox was excited by the idea of having a titled penguin in her party.

'That would be lovely,' replied Sir Olav. 'But my legs are too short to walk that far. Don't worry though – we penguins never miss a performance. There's a perfect view of the fireworks from here. We line up and enjoy every minute of it. Sometimes we can hear the bands, and sometimes we take a celebratory midnight dip after the show's over. Perhaps you'd come and join us one evening?'

'Perhaps...' said the fox. She didn't want to appear rude. 'But we had better go now. Goodbye, Sir Nils, it's been a pleasure to meet you.'

One of the Scottish Wildcats hissed and spat as they padded past. 'Just ignore him,' said the Castle Cat. 'He may be Scottish and a cat, but he is not a friend,' he added. 'A bit on the wild side.' They walked a little further. 'These, on the other hand, *are* worthy of the name 'cat'.' He strutted past the Big Cats who looked at the Castle Cat rather curiously.

'He's rather a small specimen,' muttered the lion, luckily not loud enough for the Castle Cat to hear.

By the time the fox and the cat had left the Zoo the rugby crowds had disappeared and it wasn't long before they were making their way back up the Castle rock again.

As she curled up that night the Tattoo Fox thought of Sir Nils Olav and all his penguin friends.

Edinburgh was full of lovely surprises.

7

A Magical Mystery Tour

The fox and cat head for the sea
And find a new friend up a tree

Princes Street Gardens looked magnificent with the crocuses in full bloom.

'They're such plucky little plants,' said the dog fox early one morning. 'A sure sign of spring. The weather is too good to be stuck in the den,' he continued. 'Let's see if the Castle Cat's in the mood for an outing.' He went off to find their friend and a few minutes later they returned.

'Where are we going?' asked the kits. They had only just woken up.

'Wait and see,' said their father. 'It's a Magical Mystery Tour.'

'It is not too far and all downhill,' said the cat, who was in on the secret.

The animals wove their way quickly through the New Town and down the hill towards a park where the cat suggested they stop for a rest.

'This is a huge garden,' said the Tattoo Fox gazing around.

'It's no ordinary garden,' replied the cat. 'It's the Royal Botanic Garden.' The Castle Cat loved anything to do with the Royal Family. 'Expert gardeners and botanists collect plants from all over the world and look after them here.' He glared at one of the kits who was trying to dig a plant label out of the ground. 'Please,' he said sternly, 'don't do that.'

The fox kit scampered off and hid her face in the dog fox's fur.

'That house is made of glass,' said the Tattoo Fox, changing the subject.

'That is the Palm House where they grow trees from countries that are hotter than Scotland. They keep it cosy for them. It's the tallest glass house of its kind anywhere in Great Britain,' the cat added.

They stretched out between the roots of a very tall tree with a dark red trunk and were soon drowsing in the early morning sun.

All of a sudden there was a scuffling noise above their heads. The Tattoo Fox sat up, checking on the kits who were playing a tumbling game down a nearby slope.

'Ouch!' The cat scrambled to his feet. 'We're under nut attack!'

The dog fox was being bombarded too. 'Take cover!' he cried and they all dashed beneath a shrub.

'Spoil-sports!' A red squirrel ran head first down
the tree trunk and bounded towards them. 'I know
you're in there and I promise I'll play nicely,' she
said. 'It was just too tempting...'

The fox kits emerged first. They liked the sound of
playing nicely. 'We're on a Magical Mystery Tour,'
they told her.

'But we're not stopping here,' said the cat crossly,
rubbing his head with his paw. 'That is no way to
treat guests. This is a royal garden, after all.'

'I'm sorry,' said the squirrel. Her tail drooped with embarrassment. 'You looked more fun than some of the big dogs from the houses round about. Where do you live?'

The Tattoo Fox explained that they lived by Edinburgh Castle. 'And we *are* a lot more fun than big dogs,' she agreed.

'I can see Edinburgh Castle from Inverleith Park on a fine day, but I've never visited,' said the squirrel.

'Then you must!' declared the Tattoo Fox. 'I'm having a party for the Royal Edinburgh Military Tattoo – please come. Bring a friend, if you can. The more the merrier.'

The squirrel turned in a tiny circle six times, chittering with excitement. Her tail sprang back to normal. 'Marvellous! I'd love that. I would join you on your Magical Mystery Tour, but I have to dig up the rest of my store of nuts. If I can remember where I hid them...'

'For eating, not throwing, I hope,' said the cat sharply.

'Yes, definitely,' said the squirrel. She ran back up the tree to wave them off. 'See you at the Tattoo!'

The animals set off, joining a cycle path. Most cyclists ignored them, but some stopped and took photos with their phones. The Castle Cat always showed them his best side. Before long, the Tattoo Fox picked up the smell of the sea. She looked surreptitiously at the Castle Cat but he didn't seem worried. Exactly where was this Magical Mystery Tour taking them?

The dog fox led the way towards Leith docks. The kits were nervous about the ships and machinery, but the Castle Cat explained everything. 'That one lays cables at the bottom of the sea, and those are platform supply vessels – they take food and equipment out to the oil rigs in the North Sea.'

Then they found themselves looking up at a ship so tall that they couldn't see the top of it. 'Some cruise ships like this carry more than a thousand passengers,' said the cat. 'But I have a much more special ship to show you.' They turned the corner to discover a smart ship with a dark blue hull, its white paint shining in the sunshine and lots of little flags fluttering in the breeze. 'That, my friends, was the Queen's yacht, the *Britannia*,' said the cat. He sighed. 'For forty years Her Majesty sailed the world in it. But now she is moored here and goes nowhere.' His voice was a little sad.

People were hurrying up and down the gangway carrying boxes and crates. 'That's all the food on board,' one of the men called as he jogged down the gangway. 'We'll be back this afternoon with the glasses.'

'Thanks, Ed! The band's due any time – they want to rehearse,' replied his friend. 'This is going to be quite a party.' He waved and headed back on board.

And that was when the Tattoo Fox noticed that he was not alone. Four pointed ears were following him up the gangway.

The kits!

They ignored the dog fox's first furious bark. Then the second... There was nothing else for it. Their parents would have to go and fetch them.

The two foxes and the cat crept out and along the quayside, then scurried up the gangway. They paid no attention to the beautifully laid table in the State Dining Room, and barely noticed the Queen's Sitting Room or the Royal Bedrooms. They looked everywhere – in every nook and cranny. Where were the kits?

'I hope they haven't fallen overboard,' said the Tattoo Fox.

'We'd have heard all about it if they had,' remarked the cat, shuddering. 'They can't have vanished into thin air. Let's make for the Verandah deck. Follow me!'

'Somebody's coming!' whispered the dog fox. 'Quick! In here!' The door to the Sun Lounge had been left open and they all dashed inside. A steward walked by carrying a tray of glasses, humming to herself. All of a sudden there was a mewing noise from behind one of the chairs. The two fox kits were snuggled up together, shivering with fright.

'What have I told you?' said the Tattoo Fox. 'Never ever go off on your own!' She was relieved to find them, but very cross too.

'They're safe, that's the main thing,' soothed the dog fox. He nuzzled the kits toward the doorway. 'Your mother's right,' he whispered. 'You've given us the most dreadful fright.'

The Castle Cat simply shook his head and turned on his heel. He was fond of the kits, of course, but they were a handful.

Silently, the five animals headed for the gangway. But escape wasn't to be that simple.

The Band of the Royal Marines began their rehearsal for the evening's party, including *By Land By Sea*, the bugle march named after the Royal Marines' motto, songs from all over the British Isles, a dazzling display of drumming and finally *Rule Britannia* followed by the *National Anthem*.

'Bravo!' cried the conductor when they'd finished. 'You're in excellent form.'

But one of the trombone players had caught sight of the tip of the Tattoo Fox's tail behind a curtain. 'Isn't that the fox from the Tattoo?'

71

'You're right – I'd know that tail anywhere,' said a bugler.

'Run!' barked the dog fox, and to the amazement of the band and everybody else on board the *Britannia*, *four* foxes and a large grey cat streaked past them and leapt down onto the quayside.

'Hope you enjoyed the concert!' yelled one of the trumpet players. 'Let's give them a proper send off,' he cried, and the band broke into a spirited rendition of *Life on the Ocean Wave*.

'Perhaps that wasn't the Magical Mystery Tour you imagined,' said the dog fox that evening once the fox kits were settled for the night.

'Apart from losing the kits, it was even better than I had hoped,' said the Tattoo Fox. 'Thank you.'

8

Fire!

The foxes meet a nasty rat
And stop a fire with their friend cat

Early one morning the fox family was playing among the daffodils when the Castle Cat joined them.

'Did you realise,' he asked, 'that tomorrow is the first day of summer?'

'I didn't,' admitted the Tattoo Fox. 'I'm always so busy that the changing seasons just creep up on me.'

'On the first of May people climb up Arthur's Seat at dawn to wash their faces in the dew,' said the cat. 'They believe it'll make them beautiful for the rest of the year.'

'And does it work?' asked one of the kits.

'Beauty is in the eye of the beholder,' said the cat, 'so I am sure it does work for lots of people.' He went on to explain that in many northern countries people used to light bonfires to welcome the summer. 'The soldiers are all going to the Beltane Fire Festival tonight – the night before May Day – on Calton Hill.'

'Can we go and wash our faces in the dew on the Castle Rock?' asked the kits.

'You don't need to,' said their mother, 'you look lovely already.'

'There'll be too many people, too much noise, and – worst of all – fire,' warned the cat. 'Not a place for animals.' He made it a rule to stay well away from fires these days. He would never forget the night his fur was singed by the Hogmanay fireworks.

'What about a trip underground?' the dog fox suggested. 'There are more clues to Edinburgh's history there. And later, if there's time, we'll find a hiding place on the hill and watch the Beltane Fire Festival from a safe distance.'

'Good idea! There are many old streets and abandoned homes and workshops underneath the streets,' said the cat, 'but... they are cold and dark... I don't know if the kits would like them.'

'Yes we would! Yes we would!' shouted the kits.

'We saw a ghost once – and it didn't scare us. Well, not much...' said the dog kit.

It was agreed. After lunch the friends set off using the secret routes they knew, keeping away from people and traffic. Halfway down a narrow stairway they came to a blocked off entrance. The cat slipped easily between the bars. 'This way,' he instructed. The animals squeezed through a gap in an ancient rotted wooden door and found themselves in a passageway so dark that they could not see the end. Cats and foxes can usually see quite well in the dark, and they are used to hunting at night, but there was no moonlight here.

Eventually, their eyes became accustomed to the gloom and they saw what looked like doorways to little houses leading off the narrow passageway. Everything was covered in thick dust. They walked in silence.

'People used to live and work here until the 18th Century,' whispered the cat after a while. 'But the conditions were grim and unhealthy, and gradually they moved elsewhere. Closes like this were blocked off when they began to build above,' he explained solemnly. 'I just hope they warned all the people inside to get out. I hope they found nice new homes.'

The kits stayed close by their mother's side. 'I think we've seen all we need to see,' said the Tattoo Fox, longing to be back in the fresh air.

'Me too,' said the dog fox. This wasn't quite the family outing he had imagined.

 76

'Off we go then,' said the cat, sounding enormously relieved. 'Aren't we lucky to live where we do?'

They were almost back at the entrance when out of the darkness a chilling voice cried, 'Not so fast...'

The foxes' hackles rose. They pushed the kits behind them.

A pair of red eyes glowed up at them from the end of a dripping pipe. 'What are you lot doing here?' A large black rat sidled forward. 'These are my premises and I do not appreciate trespassers noseying around,' it snapped.

The dog fox swallowed hard. 'We were just leaving. We wouldn't dream of staying where we are not welcome.'

'Then what are you waiting for?' demanded the rat rudely.

The Tattoo Fox loathed rats and didn't take her eye off it for a second. If it attacked the kits she would be ready. But the rat simply wanted them gone. 'Good riddance and don't come back,' it sneered.

Finally they slipped back through the bars and out onto the stairway.

'Thank goodness for fresh air,' said the dog fox. He gave himself an almighty shake.

'And polite company,' huffed the Castle Cat.

'I did not like that rat at all,' said one of the kits, shaking the dust out of her coat.

 78

'Not all animals are friendly. You need to learn whom to trust,' said the Tattoo Fox. 'That rat is certainly not on the guest list for my Tattoo Party.'

'Indeed not,' said the cat. 'Ill-mannered, rude, charmless, badly brought up...' He continued muttering to himself as he climbed the steps. They sheltered in a little garden beneath one of the tenements, still shocked by their underground encounter.

'Of course I would have protected you,' the Castle Cat declared. He was giving himself a thorough wash.

'Of course you would,' said the Tattoo Fox.

'Can we go home now?' asked one of the kits in a small voice. But the adventure wasn't over yet.

As they turned a corner they heard raised voices. Two boys were pushing and shoving at each other, their words taunting and harsh. 'I dare you,' the bigger of the two boys said.

'You do it!' the smaller boy retorted.

The argument must have been going on for a while.

'You're afraid, aren't you?' The bigger boy sneered. 'You're a coward!'

'No I'm not!' replied the smaller boy.

'I'll do it myself then, 'fraidy cat',' said the bigger boy.

The animals watched him pull a box of matches out of his pocket, strike one and set light to a piece of paper. As it flared up he pushed it down through a drain in the paving stones with his foot. 'There!' After a few moments tiny flames began to lick their way out of the drain. With every second that passed they grew fiercer.

'Better put it out before it gets any worse,' said the bigger boy. He didn't sound quite as pleased with himself now. The flames were getting bigger.

'How?' the smaller boy said. 'We haven't got any water.'

'Run! Let's leave it. No-one saw us. They won't know it was us...'

But the foxes and the cat had seen them, and they acted fast. While the Castle Cat ran for help, the foxes spread out and backed the boys into a corner of the close.

'Get away,' the boys shouted. They flapped their hands, but the four foxes stood their ground, growling menacingly.

'Help is on its way!' said the cat, reappearing suddenly. The flames were leaping higher and higher out of the drain now. Smoke billowed into the air. Above them people opened windows to see what was happening.

Down the close ran two policewomen, calling for the fire brigade on their radios. The boys cowered against the wall.

In a matter of minutes a team of firemen arrived, rolling their hose down the passageway. Soon they had the blaze under control. The only damage was some scorching on the stonework.

'We were lucky to catch that one in time,' said one of the firemen. 'If it had got away it could have been the Great Fire of Edinburgh. I'm not joking. Thanks for being so alert.'

'It wasn't really us,' said one of the policewomen, blushing a little. She pointed at the Castle Cat. 'He wouldn't leave us alone until we followed him down the close and – you will not believe this! – it was the foxes who detained the fire-raisers.'

The fireman raised an eyebrow.

'I know!' said the policewoman, laughing. 'It sounds crazy, but it's true. Perhaps it's a new emergency service!' She turned and pointed up the passageway. 'Right, you two – into the van before you cause any more trouble. We'll give your parents a call and then we'll have a nice long chat.' The boys sloped off, thoroughly dejected. The policewoman paused and turned to take a last look at the foxes and the cat. 'Thank you,' she said quietly. And she meant it.

Later that evening, the foxes watched the festivities on Calton Hill from their den. It was a long way off, but they were quite close enough.

'Welcome to the summer,' said the Tattoo Fox.

It had been a long day.

9

Underground Hide and Seek

The kits go up the hill to play
And find a secret passageway

'Shall I show you a great place to play Hide and Seek?' asked the cat one sunny morning, as the kits played in the courtyard outside the National War Museum.

'Yes, please,' replied the kits. 'Where?'

'Come, I will show you my special route to the Castle Vaults.'

'Will there be any rude rats there?' asked the dog kit.

'Of course not,' said the cat briskly. 'I make it my business to keep that sort of riff-raff away.' With the kits following he squeezed through a grill. 'The Vaults were built hundreds of year ago. They give Crown Square and the other castle buildings a strong foundation,' he explained, his voice echoing in the gloom.

The kits began exploring. 'What are those?' asked one. 'They look like sacks hanging up to dry.'

'Well spotted,' said the cat. 'These vaults were prisons in the old days, and those are hammocks where the prisoners slept. There were Frenchmen and Americans, Spanish, Germans, Italians, Dutch, Danish, Irish and even an Icelander or two. Fights often broke out – 'my country's better than yours' sort of thing – but when they were not squabbling, they made things out of wood and bedstraw and meat bones and sold them to visitors. Some of the craftier ones even tried to forge banknotes.'

'I would not like to be a prisoner down here,' said the smaller kit.

'Indeed,' agreed the cat. 'But it's the perfect place for Hide and Seek these days. We'll count to fifty – off you go!'

The kit dashed out of sight and once they were ready the cat and the dog kit started to search through all the rooms, under beds, inside hammocks and behind cupboards – but there was no sign of her.

After a while the Castle Cat became slightly alarmed but tried not show it. The dog kit happily went on looking for his sister. Finally the cat called, 'Time to go! The Castle opens to visitors in a few minutes!' He waited.

There was an eerie silence. The cat's tail twitched. 'We'll have to leave her for now,' he said tersely. 'I'll take you back to your den, then return to find your naughty sister.' But as the cat and the kit were heading towards the grill they heard a scratching sound and turned to see the missing kit skipping towards them covered in dirt and cobwebs.

'Where have you been?' asked the cat.

'I found a tunnel which goes on for miles and miles,' she said, her eyes shining. 'When I came to a place where a lot of rubble had fallen in I thought I should come back.'

The cat narrowed his eyes. 'A tunnel?' he said. 'One of the stewards says there's a tunnel leading all the way from Edinburgh Castle down to the Queen's Palace at Holyrood. I wonder whether that's the one.'

'Shall we go back and see?' asked the kit.

'No,' replied the cat firmly. 'Not with visitors about.'

Once they were out in the fresh air, the dog kit laughed at his sister. 'You look like a ghost covered in all that white dust. You should go back and scare people!'

'That is quite enough silliness for today,' said the cat, hurrying them round the back of the barracks towards the tunnel. As they emerged onto the Esplanade a large coach drove up, full of visitors. They caught sight of the animals and started to take photographs and for once the cat was reluctant to pose. He was in a hurry to return the kits safely to their parents. But as they slipped through the railings he heard the tour leader calling, 'This way! The Assembly Halls are on The Mound. That's where we'll see Prince Edward!'

What was going on? Why were tourists heading *away* from the Castle? And Prince Edward was a member of the Royal Family. Why on earth did the Castle Cat know nothing of his arrival? There was no time to lose. He hurried the kits away.

The Tattoo Fox scolded the little kit for getting so dirty and causing such worry. 'What have I said about getting lost?' she reminded her.

 88

'Well, to be fair, getting lost is the point of Hide and Seek,' the cat mentioned.

'I found a secret tunnel,' said the kit. 'I'll show it to you one day,' she offered.

The Tattoo Fox couldn't help being proud of her kits. They were growing up fast. 'Thank you for looking after them,' she said to the cat. 'You look as if you're in a hurry.'

'I am,' he replied. 'There is something going on at the Assembly Halls that I absolutely must investigate. It involves a member of the Royal Family.'

'Can I come too?' asked the Tattoo Fox.

'I'll look after the kits,' offered the dog fox, happy to be left behind. He wasn't a big fan of the Royal Family. He'd heard ugly rumours about their attitude to foxes.

The cat and the fox ran along Ramsay Garden towards the Mound until they reached a patch of grass. Two crows were sitting squawking to each other. They shuffled a little nervously at first, but when it was clear this wasn't a hunting expedition, the four of them began chatting.

'Today is the start of the General Assembly of the Church of Scotland,' explained one of the crows. 'What a thrill! We come every year. Some of the most colourful people in the country will be parading.'

'Who is that man carrying the big sword and who are all those people following him?' asked the fox, intrigued.

'That is the ceremonial sword of this great city,' said the cat quickly. He didn't want the crows to think he knew nothing. 'It was given to the city by King Charles the First and it is being carried by one of the City Officers. Behind him, wearing those heavy gold chains, are all the Lord and Lady Provosts and Conveners of the Councils from all over Scotland. The men and women with them are the chief officials of each council.'

They watched as the dignitaries walked up the long stairway to the Assembly Hall.

'Now come the heads of the Navy, the Army and the Air Force in Scotland. They're wearing their best uniforms,' the cat continued.

'And here come our favourites,' said the crows, stamping from foot to foot with excitement. 'What a thrill!'

The fox had never seen anything like it. 'Who are those people in their gloriously coloured coats?'

Before the crows had time to explain, the cat did. 'That is the Lord Lyon. He's in charge of all of the most important state ceremonies in Scotland and he is not wearing a coat,' he said with pompous precision. 'He is wearing a tabard.'

'He doesn't look like a lion to me,' the fox observed.

'It's Lyon with a 'y' not an 'i',' said the cat sharply, 'and he is the most important Herald in the country. The others wearing tabards are all heralds.'

'We love a bit of tradition,' chirruped one of the crows. 'There's The Lord High Constable, the Master of the Royal Household, the Bearer of the Royal Banner, the Bearer of the National Flag and the Purse Bearer.'

The cat blinked. These crows certainly knew a thing or too. A beautifully polished car with no number-plates drew up and Prince Edward, the Earl of Wessex, climbed out and waved to the crowds. As he climbed the steps the State Trumpeters blew a welcoming fanfare.

'What a thrill!' The crows bounced and flapped with excitement.

'Prince Edward must be The Lord High Commissioner this year,' announced the cat. 'That means he's the Queen's representative at the General Assembly of the Church of Scotland.'

'So the Queen isn't coming?' The fox was a little disappointed.

'No – but she'll be visiting in July,' squawked the crows.

'I look forward to that,' said the fox. And before she and the cat set off back towards the castle she invited the crows to her Tattoo Party.

'We'd love to come! What a thrill!'

10

Another Castle, Another Time

**The fox thinks she will watch a show
And sees a Queen from long ago**

The Tattoo Fox loved listening to the stories the tour guides told. She had learnt about Scotland's history from them – and the Castle Cat, of course.

She often heard them mention Craigmillar Castle, and one evening the Castle Cat explained how to get there. 'I'd come with you,' he said. 'But they're delivering the stands for the Tattoo in the next few days. Somebody needs to be here to keep an eye on things.' He was rather grumpy because he had discovered there were to be pop concerts at the Castle again that July. He was not a fan of pop concerts. The Tattoo Fox rather enjoyed them – and especially the snacks the audience left behind.

The following morning the Tattoo Fox set off. The kits would be busy doing pouncing practice with their father for the rest of the day. She skirted round the east side of Arthur's Seat to avoid the runners puffing through the park. By the time she had reached the far side of the hill she was a little out of breath and paused for a drink at Dunsapie Loch, disturbing some swans who angrily chased her away. She made a dash for Prestonfield Golf Course and from there she darted across a wide road and through a sports ground. Soon she was looking up at the ruins of Craigmillar Castle.

It was full of people. Some of them were putting on strange clothes. One lady was wearing a long black dress with a fine lace ruff around her throat. She looked most unusual.

'Hello, can I help?'

The fox turned to find a large hare regarding her from a distance. His voice was friendly but he was taking no chances. 'You gave me quite a fright,' the fox said. 'I was just wondering what was going on.'

'You do not live here, then,' said the hare.

'No,' replied the fox. She explained that she lived beneath Edinburgh Castle.

'This is a different kind of castle,' said the hare. 'Let me tell you about it.'

The fox and the hare circled the castle, keeping out of sight. The hare pointed out the Tower House. 'It's four storeys high,' he explained. 'There is a hall, and a kitchen, and guard rooms and bedrooms. Lots of little nooks and crannies to explore when there is nobody around,' he added.

'My kits would love it here,' said the fox. 'But what are these people doing?' More and more of them were changing into strange clothes.

'They are actors and they are going to tell a story about one of the most famous visitors to Craigmillar Castle,' the hare replied.

'I love stories, especially stories from history,'
said the fox.

'This story happened hundreds of years ago, when
Craigmillar Castle was much smaller. Famous
people used to come here to escape prying eyes in
the city,' the hare said. 'People were very
suspicious of each other. The royal household was
particularly unhappy. The lady in the black dress is
playing the part of Mary, Queen of Scots. She came
here to get away from her husband, Lord Darnley.'

In the West Garden the actors were preparing to
perform in the bright sunshine. The hare and the
fox found a safe place from which to watch. Before
long, the fox was lost in the story. She had never
seen anything like it.

As the afternoon went on, the castle seemed to
change. It looked less crumbly, and the gardens
were now neatly planted with flowers. The
beautiful Queen looked sad as she walked with
her host, Sir Simon Preston. She was speaking
with a French accent, telling him how nervous and
lonely she was. 'I can trust nobody. I miss David so
much. He was loyal, such a good friend,' she said.

'Riccio's murder must have been a terrible shock,' said Sir Simon. He assured her of his continuing protection and loyalty. 'We have known each other for such a long time,' he continued. 'You know you can trust me.'

The Tattoo Fox remembered a story the Castle Cat had told her, of the brutal murder of David Riccio, the Queen's secretary, in Holyrood Palace.

The Queen and Sir Simon continued to walk in silence, until four women – the Queen's ladies-in-waiting – entered the garden. One of them was carrying a howling baby. 'Your Royal Highness,' said the lady-in-waiting, 'he wants his maman.' She handed the baby to the Queen, and he immediately quietened and smiled up at her.

'He is always happier away from the Palace of Holyroodhouse,' the Queen told Sir Simon. 'Away from Lord Darnley.' She hugged the baby to her, then thanked Sir Simon for his company and walked with her son and ladies-in-waiting back to the Castle.

The fox shook her head. The castle now looked as it had when she arrived. 'It's as if I was in a strange dream,' she said. 'So much unhappiness. How sad the Queen was.'

'It all happened nearly four hundred and fifty years ago,' said the hare. 'There is nothing we can do about it now. Mary Queen of Scots had a very sad life in many ways. I like to think Craigmillar Castle was one of the places she was happiest.'

The audience was leaving and the actors were packing away their costumes, laughing and chatting. Everything was back to normal.

'I should go,' said the fox. 'But thank you. Please accept my invitation to the Tattoo Party. If you wouldn't mind coming into the centre of the city, I think you would enjoy it very much. There are bands and pipers and dancers and singers. It's noisy, but great fun.'

'I often watch the Tattoo fireworks from here,'
said the hare. 'It would be wonderful to see them
up close. And I love music. Yes please, I would
love to come.'

The Tattoo Fox gave one last look at Craigmillar
Castle. Like so many places in Edinburgh, it had
its ghosts. She trotted down the hill, making her
way home back to her den.

11

The Uninvited Guests

The Tattoo Fox fulfils her dream
When at last she meets the Queen

One morning the Castle Cat arrived at the foxes'
den at quite a speed. 'I have exciting news!' he said.

The foxes rushed to greet him. The kits were
almost as big as their parents these days.

'The soldiers are preparing for the Queen's visit.
They say that she will be here next week,' he
announced.

'Is she visiting Edinburgh Castle?' asked the
Tattoo Fox.

'No,' said the cat, 'so we will visit her.'

'I'm happy to stay here with the kits,' said the dog fox quickly. The kits were big enough to be left on their own, but everybody knew he wanted an excuse to stay at home.

'Just us, then!' said the cat cheerfully. 'Like old times. I'll make a plan. In the meantime, make sure your coat is as clean and shiny as possible, and your tail fluffy and groomed.'

Two evenings later the cat came to tell the fox to be ready the following day. The fox could hardly sleep for excitement and was ready long before the Castle Cat arrived, looking very smart with his fur groomed, his whiskers straightened and his paws clean. It was a sunny day as the two friends set off by their secret ways and emerged close to the Canongate, at the foot of the Royal Mile. Police and traffic wardens were lining up barriers along the road.

'What's going on?' asked the fox. 'Isn't it time you explained?'

'Very well.' The cat purred louder than ever before. 'Today the Queen is holding a party in the garden of the Palace of Holyroodhouse and there will be thousands of guests. Her Garden Parties are wonderful occasions. But we must be careful that we are not spotted and chased away.'

A Japanese tourist took a photo of them with his mobile phone and showed it to all his friends.

'That's not a terribly good start,' said the cat frostily, and stalked off towards the Scottish Parliament building. They sat and watched the Palace from beside a shrub.

'Quick!' said the cat suddenly. A catering van had just arrived with food for the Garden Party and a policeman was opening the gate to let it in. The two friends sprinted through behind the van, unnoticed.

'Excellent!' said the cat, his spirits restored.

Men and women in smart aprons were setting up tables inside two long open-fronted tents. Others brought glasses and cups and saucers, and piles of small plates. They set out platters of little sandwiches and cakes for all the Queen's guests. In two little pavilions at opposite ends of the garden some military bandsmen were tuning their instruments, putting up their music stands and arranging their seats.

'Marvellous!' said the cat. He loved the sound of bands. 'Now, let's make sure that we have a good view.' The two friends prowled the flowerbeds to find the best place to hide, and the best place from which to see the Queen.

A man was gently knocking slender stakes into the grass with a mallet. 'That's my good friend Mr

Tymoczko, The Officer from the Royal Company of Archers,' said the cat. 'He's marking out two avenues for the Royal Family to walk down. Guests form a line down either side hoping the Queen – or one of her family – will say hello on the way to their tea tent. The Archers maintain order.'

'Will they fire arrows if people misbehave?' asked the fox.

'People usually behave at the Queen's Garden Parties,' the cat reassured her.

All of a sudden there was a terrific sound of sniffing and snorting and a dog pushed his way through the undergrowth, stopping just in front of them. With a hiss, the cat dived deep into the shrubbery, but the fox stood her ground. The dog looked strangely familiar.

'I don't believe it!' he wuffed. 'Of all the foxes in all the world, it's the Tattoo Fox!' His tail wagged in circles. 'How have you been?'

The fox gave a shake of relief. Of course! It was the sniffer dog she'd met last summer at the Tattoo. After a prickly start they had become good friends.

'We've come to see the Queen,' she said. 'Please don't give us away.'

'Of course I won't! *You* are alright. But was that a *cat* I saw with you?'

'I am the Castle Cat,' the cat replied, emerging from a shrub as if he hadn't been in the least scared.

'That's fine, just don't cause any trouble,' the sniffer dog replied cheerfully. 'Better head off. Lots of royal garden to check. I'm extremely busy. My handler has exceptionally high standards. Oh, and a tip for you – the guests have trouble drinking their tea and eating their sandwiches and cakes at the same time, so there's always lots of food dropped on the ground.' He winked and rushed off.

'That dog is a little uncouth,' said the cat. 'But it was good of him to tell us about the food.'

'I didn't get a chance to invite him to the Tattoo Party!' exclaimed the fox. She hoped he'd be back.

Soon people began to stroll round the garden. They were all smartly dressed. Most of the ladies wore fancy hats with their summer dresses. Some wobbled on very high heels. A few men wore top hats and tail coats, and others wore kilts or tartan trews. But the fox and the cat were particularly interested in the guests wearing their national costumes.

'They are from different Commonwealth countries,' explained the cat.

'It's the Commonwealth Games soon,' the fox said. 'They must be here for that.'

'The Commonwealth Games are in Glasgow,' said the cat, as if that might be a problem.

'There are trains from Waverley Station every fifteen minutes,' the fox reminded him. She wouldn't mind going there one of these days.

The bands struck up, first one and then the other. The Castle Cat was in his element as they played all his favourite show tunes. Suddenly a hush fell over the crowd and the fox saw a door open at the top of an iron stairway leading from the palace.

'She's here!' cried the cat and immediately stood to attention.

Through the doorway walked the Queen, followed by other members of the royal family. They all waited while the nearest band played the National Anthem. Then the Queen made her way down into the garden, walking slowly along one of the avenues chatting to the guests. The avenues led to the Royal Tea Tent and the Archers stood round in a circle so that people could see the Queen and her guests – but from a distance.

'Isn't she magnificent?' said the Castle Cat dreamily.

'I'm going to have a closer look,' decided the fox.

'Don't be silly,' the cat hissed. 'We're not exactly on the royal guest list.'

But the fox's mind was made up. She darted out of the bushes onto the lawn, winding through the legs of the guests and towards the royal tea tent. The cat followed. He couldn't possibly leave her unprotected, after all.

The royal guests were enjoying their tea and sandwiches. They chatted about this and that, and commented on the warm weather, a perfect day for a Royal Garden Party. Suddenly a beautiful fox and a handsome cat appeared on the grass in front of the tent. There was a moment's hush and then people began to laugh and applaud as the fox walked forward and bowed to the Queen. The cat wasn't going to be left out. He followed and bowed too, purring loudly. The Queen looked round and smiled broadly at her guests. Then the fox and the cat sprinted back the way they had come.

One of the Archers said to another, 'Should we have stopped them?'

'Probably, but they were very polite. And they can move faster than we can.' The two men laughed. They were trained for many emergencies, but not that one.

The Tattoo Fox and the Castle Cat lay flat under the bush, jubilant. Before long a familiar sniffing and snorting alerted them to the arrival of the sniffer dog.

'You pair take the biscuit!' he yapped, running round in circles again. 'My handler couldn't believe his eyes.'

'Nor could we,' said the fox. She was quite shocked at her bold behaviour. But she had no regrets.

'I can't believe you did that! Better dash!' The dog turned to go but the fox stopped him.

'Can you come to my Tattoo Party?' she asked.

'Try stopping me!' he replied, his tail going nineteen to the dozen. 'See you on the Esplanade!' And he scuttled off to do more important sniffing.

'Let's head home,' the Castle Cat said. 'I think I've had enough excitement for one day.' The two friends ran through the Abbey and under the gates onto the Abbey Strand.

'I am sorry we didn't get any of the leftover cakes and sandwiches,' said the fox as they trotted towards the Castle, 'but it was lovely to meet the Queen. I will remember her smile for ever.'

12

A Party to Remember

The fox's friends each come to call
This year's Tattoo will thrill them all

It wasn't long before the first of the Tattoo
performers arrived at the Esplanade to rehearse.
They marched and played until a man in a white
hat told them it was time for the next group to
take their place. Each time they practised, their
performances improved. 'I think this year's Tattoo
might be even better than last year's,' said the
dog fox, watching from beneath the stands.

'It's dress rehearsal night tomorrow,' said the
Castle Cat. 'Can't wait. I'm off for an early night so
that I'll be ready to enjoy it tomorrow.'

That night there was a lighting rehearsal. The people who operated the spotlights and the coloured lights had a very complicated job. They prided themselves on getting it right, night after night. But things were not going smoothly. It was wet and windy, and everybody was rather anxious.

'Don't worry,' said the Producer, huddled under his umbrella. 'Let's give it another go.'

The engineers ran up and down the gantries replacing bulbs and shifting the huge lights, determined to make everything perfect. Finally, in the early hours of the morning, they were happy with the results.

'Bravo,' said the Producer. 'Well done, everybody!' Then he caught sight of the white tip of a fox's tail disappearing under the stands. 'She's back,' he said to himself. 'Our Tattoo Fox has returned.' And he smiled as he headed down Castlehill with the rest of the team.

But just by the Camera
Obscura a huge gust
of wind took them all by
surprise. It whisked the
Producer's folder into the air and
off into the night. He could only
watch helplessly as his notes flew out
over the Esplanade into the driving rain.
Everybody tried to grab them, but it was no use.

'Don't worry,' said the Producer's colleague. 'We'll
print another Running Order off tomorrow.'

The Producer thanked her and said, 'Let's go home
now, we've got a big day ahead.' He tried to sound
cheerful, but his heart was heavy. His Running
Order had been covered in his pencil notes. He
would never remember them all. He tried not to
think about it as he drove home that night.

In the morning, the kits reported that the
Esplanade was a mess. 'There is litter
everywhere,' they said, outraged.

'That's strange,' said their mother. She went to take a look. The bits of paper were a bit damp and she couldn't read what was written on them, of course, but they didn't look like litter. These weren't chocolate wrappers or sandwich boxes or discarded receipts. She began to gather them up, one by one. The kits came and joined her, and they did their bit. The dog fox came too, once he'd caught breakfast. By the time the foxes had finished, they had quite a pile of paper. But what should they do with it now?

'Run and get the Castle Cat, he'll know what to do.'

The cat looked long and hard at the pile of paper. Finally he said, 'It says 'Producer's Tattoo Running Order'. I can't read it all,' he admitted, 'but it must be important.'

There was a snorting and a sniffing and the sniffer dog came careering towards them. 'Can't stop!' he said. 'Terribly busy!' He gave the pile of papers a passing sniff. 'These belong to the Producer,' he said, screeching to a halt. 'What on earth are *you* doing with them?'

The fox told him the whole story.

'Well, a gold star to the lot of you,' said the sniffer dog. 'This is vital stuff. Don't go away!' He hurried off.

The sniffer dog's handler was in a meeting. 'I'm afraid my notes were blown away last night,' the Producer was explaining, 'and I'm sure you all know exactly what you're doing, but I am rather worried.' He looked pale. He hadn't slept well.

'The dogs have security covered,' said the handler. 'So you can...' He stopped. His dog was not out in the stands where he was supposed to be, sniffing out trouble. He was here in the meeting, snuffling at his handler's hand. 'What are you doing here?' he muttered. But the dog wouldn't leave him alone. 'If you'll excuse me,' the handler said and jogged out of the meeting after the dog. At the far end of the Esplanade the sniffer dog stopped, and the handler saw what looked like four foxes disappearing behind a stairway. A large grey cat was standing next to a pile of paper, holding it down with one large paw.

The cat removed his paw so that the handler could pick up the papers. 'Incredible! I do believe you've saved the day,' said the handler, scratching the dog's ears. 'And you,' he said to the cat. 'And you!' he called to where he thought the four foxes were hiding.

The Producer was overjoyed when the handler dashed back into the meeting waving the lost notes. They were rather wrinkly and still a little damp, but once he'd put them in the right order he felt much better. The Dress Rehearsal went like a dream and, as the Producer told his wife when he got home that night, he was sure that the Tattoo Fox had something to do with it.

The opening night of the Royal Edinburgh Military Tattoo was a triumph. People from all over the world roared and cheered, though some wept during the lone piper's lament, as they always did. There was something for everybody and they all went home humming and dancing, overjoyed by the whole experience. For three weeks the performances continued, with every seat taken. For three weeks the Tattoo Fox watched every performance, often joined by her family. The Tattoo was every bit as thrilling as the previous year.

On the final night she waited for her guests to arrive.

First came the Dundas Castle Fox, trotting up the rock from Princes Street Gardens. He and the dog fox discovered they had a lot in common.

Then came Myrtle. She was wearing a smart new tartan collar.

The crows arrived looking particularly shiny. 'What a thrill!' they squawked as they landed by the foxes' den. And they kept squawking 'What a thrill!' for the rest of the evening.

The hare was a little shy and hid behind a tree until the Tattoo Fox spotted him. 'Come away in,' she said. 'I've told everybody about you!' It wasn't long before the hare and the Castle Cat were enthusiastically exchanging fascinating facts.

The red squirrel arrived a little late – she'd been distracted by some fat balls in a garden in Inverleith. But she was soon the life and soul of the party. And she'd brought some friends. The Castle

Cat was doubtful about them at first, concerned that they might throw things at the performers. But he needn't have worried. They behaved perfectly.

The sniffer dog was the last to join them. 'Done some serious sniffing tonight,' he explained. 'But I'm off duty for the rest of the show.'

The Tattoo Fox welcomed them all and introduced them to her family and to each other. 'You are my new friends,' she said proudly. 'Welcome to our Tattoo Party!'

The sniffer dog led them all to a secret hideout with the best views over the Esplanade towards the Castle. They were all enthralled by the whole spectacle of the Tattoo with its sparkling lights and colourful costumes, its glorious music and dazzling fireworks. The Tattoo Fox thought of Sir Nils Olav and the other penguins enjoying the bright colours and startling shapes in the sky. All her new friends were having a wonderful time.

They were entranced by the Lone Piper high on the battlements and spellbound by the storyteller reciting Sir Walter Scott's poetry. Then the Scott-Barrett rocket fired high into the night sky and the cast of the Royal Edinburgh Military Tattoo began to march away for the last time.

But the show wasn't yet over. The Dundas Castle Fox, Myrtle the Terrier, the squirrel, the crows and the hare couldn't believe their eyes.

Behind the Pipes and Drums marched the Tattoo Fox, her beautiful tail held high.

'Would you believe it!' barked the sniffer dog, his tail beating in time to the music. 'There goes our Tattoo Fox!'

From their box up in the stands, the Producer and the Storyteller smiled and clapped along with the audience as the Tattoo Fox marched out of the Esplanade and into the night.

ALASDAIR HUTTON has enjoyed writing little stories since he was a child. The first Tattoo Fox book was such fun to create that he happily agreed to write some more adventures with the same characters.

He has written and presented the Royal Edinburgh Military Tattoo since 1992 along with hundreds of other tattoos and concerts around the world.

Formerly a journalist and broadcaster, Territorial Army paratrooper, Member of the European Parliament and local councillor, Alasdair is now active in charity work, especially raising money for ex-service men and women.

Alasdair lives in the Scottish border town of Kelso and has two grown-up sons and a grand-daughter who lives far away in America and for whom he loves writing stories.

STEPHEN WHITE lives in Edinburgh and works under the pen-name Stref. He has worked with DC Thomson for many years, producing work for their comic publications, *The Dandy* and *The Beano*. Characters he has drawn include Dennis The Menace, The Bash Street Kids, Minnie The Minx, Billy Whizz, Desperate Dan, Winker Watson, Brassneck, Keyhole Kate, Dreadlock Holmes and many others. He also works on Sunday Post characters Oor Wullie and The Broons. Stephen has had two graphic novels published independently, and a collection of newspaper style cartoon strips, called *Raising Amy*. He is currently working on his fourth book, a faithful graphic novel adaptation of J M Barrie's *Peter Pan*, due out in 2015.

The Tattoo Fox
Alasdair Hutton
With illustrations by Stref
ISBN 9781908373939
PBK £5.99

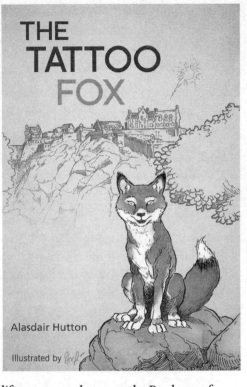

The Tattoo was a brilliant sight
The fox came back there every night

A little fox makes her home by Edinburgh Castle and with the help of her new friend, the Castle Cat, she settles in well. But there is one question the Castle Cat refuses to answer. What is the Tattoo?

'Just wait and see,' he tells her.

Will she ever find out?

This heart-warming tale was inspired by a real-life encounter between the Producer of the Royal Edinburgh Military Tattoo and a fox, late one night on the Castle Esplanade.

Let's Explore Edinburgh Old Town

Anne Bruce English
Illustrations by Cinders McLeod
ISBN 9780946487981 PBK £4.99

 The Old Town of Edinburgh has everything. At the highest point is a huge castle. At the foot of the hill there's a palace.

Between them are secret gardens, a museum full of toys, a statue of the world famous Greyfriars Bobby, and much more besides.

There were murders here too (think of Burke and Hare). There's mystery – is preacher John Knox really buried under parking space 44? And then there are the ghosts of Mary King's Close.

You can find out about all this and more in this guide. Read the tales of the Old Town, check out the short quizzes and the Twenty Questions page (all the answers are given), and you'll have plenty to see and do. Join Anne and Cinders on a fascinating and fun journey through time.

Wild Lives: Foxes: The Blood is Wild

Bridget MacCaskill
ISBN 9780946487714 PBK £9.99

 In the endless struggle between man and nature, Bridget and Don MacCaskill's Highland home has always been a haven for injured and orphaned wildlife, from red deer to wildcats. The story begins with the rescue of two near-starved fox cubs called Rufus and Rusty, victims of their species' vicious reputation, and charts their often amusing journey into adulthood under the watchful eye of their new human 'parents'. Along the way, they are regularly joined by other wild creatures in need of the MacCaskills' help – badgers, birds of prey and a majestic golden eagle among them. *The Blood is Wild* is a touching account of the precarious existence of wildlife in the Highlands.

Details of these and other books published by Luath Press can be found at: **www.luath.co.uk**

Luath Press Limited

committed to publishing well written books worth reading

LUATH PRESS takes its name from Robert Burns, whose little collie Luath (*Gael.*, swift or nimble) tripped up Jean Armour at a wedding and gave him the chance to speak to the woman who was to be his wife and the abiding love of his life. Burns called one of 'The Twa Dogs' Luath after Cuchullin's hunting dog in Ossian's *Fingal*. Luath Press was established in 1981 in the heart of Burns country, and now resides a few steps up the road from Burns' first lodgings on Edinburgh's Royal Mile.

Luath offers you distinctive writing with a hint of unex-pected pleasures.

Most bookshops in the UK, the US, Canada, Australia, New Zealand and parts of Europe either carry our books in stock or can order them for you. To order direct from us, please send a £sterling cheque, postal order, international money order or your credit card details (number, address of cardholder and expiry date) to us at the address below. Please add post and packing as follows: UK – £1.00 per delivery address; overseas surface mail – £2.50 per delivery address; overseas airmail – £3.50 for the first book to each delivery address, plus £1.00 for each additional book by airmail to the same address. If your order is a gift, we will happily enclose your card or message at no extra charge.

Luath Press Limited
543/2 Castlehill
The Royal Mile
Edinburgh EH1 2ND
Scotland
Telephone: 0131 225 4326 (24 hours)
Fax: 0131 225 4324
email: sales@luath.co.uk
Website: www.luath.co.uk